For my mother, Judith & my pops, Big Tony — Z.A.

Special thanks to: Yasemin Uçar, Elena Giovinazzo & Marie Bartholomew

Published in Canada and the U.S. by Kids Can Press Ltd.
25 Dockside Drive, Toronto, ON M5A 0B5

Kids Can Press is a Corus Entertainment Inc. company

www.kidscanpress.com

The artwork in this book was rendered in pencil and gouache.
The text is set in Andis.

Edited by Yasemin Uçar
Designed by Marie Bartholomew

Printed and bound in Buji, Shenzhen, China, in 10/2021
by WKT Company

CM 22 0 9 8 7 6 5 4 3 2 1

FSC
www.fsc.org
MIX
Paper from
responsible sources
FSC® C010256

Library and Archives Canada Cataloguing in Publication
Title: Clementine and the lion / Zoey Abbott.
Names: Abbott, Zoey, author, illustrator.
Identifiers: Canadiana 20210210354 | ISBN 9781525305627 (hardcover)
Classification: LCC PZ7.1.A23 Cl 2022 | DDC j813/.6 — dc23

Kids Can Press gratefully acknowledges that the land on which our office is located is the traditional territory of many nations, including the Mississaugas of the Credit, the Anishnabeg, the Chippewa, the Haudenosaunee and the Wendat peoples, and is now home to many diverse First Nations, Inuit and Métis peoples.

We thank the Government of Ontario, through Ontario Creates; the Ontario Arts Council; the Canada Council for the Arts; and the Government of Canada for supporting our publishing activity.

CLEMENTINE
AND THE LION

Zoey ABBOTT

Kids Can Press

Clementine's mother and father
looked like normal, everyday parents,
but they were not.
   They were ogres of the worst kind.

So one day, when her mother was
snatched by dragons and her father
was lost at sea in a bottle ...

Clementine found herself rather relieved to be alone (with Blue Bear, of course).

She ate when and where she pleased.

She sang to the plants for hours.

She did her hair as she liked,
or not, depending on her mood.
Clementine was happy.

That is, until Aunt Mildred
showed up to "take care of her."

IF I WORE MY HAIR
LIKE YOURS, PEOPLE WOULD
THINK I WAS A WITCH.

Clementine didn't
think it mattered much
how Aunt Mildred wore
her hair.

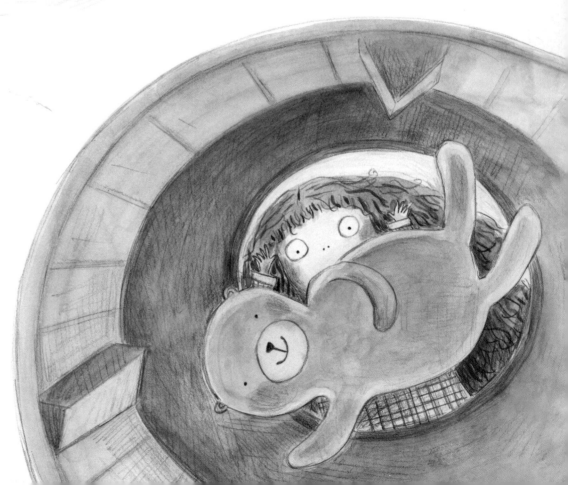

That night, Clementine began experimenting with a recipe for invisibility paint.

The next morning, it was just right.

When Aunt Mildred was out shopping,
Clementine set to work.

When Aunt Mildred
returned, there was
nothing she could do
but leave.

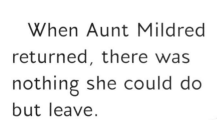

Soon, everyone forgot about Clementine.

Clementine learned to take good care of herself.

FIVE SAUSAGES AND SIXTEEN SLICES OF BOLOGNA, PLEASE.

She exercised daily.

She took ample quiet time.

She came up with her
own ways of doing things.

And she was always
careful to sneak in and
out of the house when
no one was looking.

But one afternoon,
with both arms full of
groceries, Clementine left
the door open a crack.

Then, when she was
done putting everything
away, she turned to find ...

a most terrifying and uninvited guest.

Clementine fled for the nearest cupboard.

She waited.

She listened.

And she wondered ...

What on earth was
going on in her home?

When Clementine was
sure the beast was asleep,
she crept out of the
cupboard to have a look.
   The food was gone.
   The place was a wreck.

Clementine realized there
was nothing she could do
but leave.

But *wait*.

Where was ...?

Clementine couldn't leave without ...

It was then that Clementine decided she was done
with being invisible. She was going to stay after all.

And if the guest also wanted to stick around, they were going to have to learn to live with each other.

So the lion followed Clementine's lead.

And she followed his.

Clementine's parents would be able to find their way home.

Ceci n'est pas
un peigne.